P9-CFS-398

To:

From:

To Meagan and Linley, with all my love. —GEL

With love for my dad, who is always there for me in every way that matters most, and for my boys, Jon and Justin, the best sons I can imagine. —SLH

For Mya. —SH

Why a Daughter Needs a Dad copyright © 2004, 2019 by Gregory E. Lang
Text adapted for picture book by Susanna Leonard Hill
Cover and internal illustrations copyright © 2019 by Sydney Hanson
Cover and internal design by Sourcebooks

Sourcebooks and the colophon are registered trademarks of Sourcebooks.

All rights reserved.

The art was sketched with pencil and colored pencil, then scanned and painted digitally.

Published by Sourcebooks Jabberwocky, an imprint of Sourcebooks
P.O. Box 4410, Naperville, Illinois 60567-4410
(630) 961-3900
sourcebooks.com

Library of Congress Cataloging-in-Publication Data is on file with the publisher.

Source of Production: Worzalla, Stevens Point, Wisconsin, USA
Date of Production: August 2021
Run Number: 5022860
Printed and bound in the United States of America.
WOZ 10

Why a Daughter Needs a Dad

by Gregory E. Lang   pictures by Sydney Hanson

Adapted for picture book by Susanna Leonard Hill

sourcebooks
jabberwocky

From the first time I held you, so perfect and new,

I promised to do everything that I could do

to help you become your most wonderful YOU,

my darling, my daughter, my girl.

Artistic, athletic, determined and smart,

honest and brave, with a kind, loving heart.

It's what's *in*side that matters and sets you apart.

Be true to yourself, precious girl.

No one starts out knowing all there is to know.

We all make mistakes as we struggle to grow.

What matters is trying to learn as you go.

Beside you, I'll guide you, my girl.

I'll urge you to give taking first steps a try.

You'll climb on the school bus and I'll wave goodbye.

I'll let go of your two-wheeler and watch you fly.

But I'll always be right here for you.

When mind-spinning questions keep you up at night,

I'll answer them all and then tuck you in tight.

I'll make certain you know everything is all right.

Sleep soundly, dream sweetly, my girl.

You can go off and play after school with a friend,

or visit your grandparents for the weekend,

or wander the wide world from end to far end…

Home will always be waiting for you.

I'll help you be honest in all that you do,

for being untruthful will catch up with you.

No one wants friends they can't trust to be true,

so be strong and upstanding, my girl.

When your friend scores a goal and you just do okay,

or someone else gets the lead role in the play,

I'll help you remember that you'll have your day

to come out on top, my sweet girl.

Remember that anything you choose to do

will have an effect on the world around you.

Before you take action, please think your way through

and make thoughtful decisions, my girl.

There are times when a girl needs her dad's warm embrace,

a shoulder to cry on, a judgment-free space,

someone who can put the smile on her face.

I'll always be here for my girl.

The world is a mix—ever-changing and new—

of people who look and act different from you,

who may not believe the same things that you do,

but be open to difference, my girl.

You'll master some skills, solve some problems with ease,

but others may wrestle you down to your knees.

I'll help you to try 'til you gain expertise.

Keep at it! You'll get it, my girl.

Look out for people, and animals too,

younger or smaller or weaker than you.

Be one who helps—someone they can turn to,

my kind and responsible girl.

Although as you grow you'll have fun things to do,

school days and friendships, activities too,

make time for your family—the ones who love you.

Family first and forever, sweet girl.

I'll cheer your accomplishments, little and great,

share all the proud moments you earn and create,

be glad for your triumphs and joys—celebrate!—

and hope life's full of wonder for you.

I love you for all that you are and will be,

for everything good you have given to me.

You make me the father I hoped I would be,

my darling, my daughter, my world.